Vanessa and Johnny

Vanessa and Johnny

The Cabinets

Whitney Lauren

Order this book online at www.trafford.com
or email orders@trafford.com

Most Trafford titles are also available at major online book retailers.

Printed in the United States of America.

ISBN: 978-1-4269-5827-4 (sc)
ISBN: 978-1-4269-5828-1 (e)

Library of Congress Control Number: 2011902486

Trafford rev.03/21/2011

 www.trafford.com

North America & International
toll-free: 1 888 232 4444 (USA & Canada)
phone: 250 383 6864 ♦ fax: 812 355 4082

Chapter 1

Since my first day at Book Smith Elementary School I've had the honor of being assigned to teachers with one or two screws loose—I was even sure that some of them had a whole set of screws missing! But thanks to my school's class exchange program for fifth graders, I was stuck with having not one but *three* teachers with a couple of cuckoo birds up in the nest. Principal Westler said he wanted to give us older kids a chance to stretch our legs more. *Whatever.* If only he knew that my homeroom teacher, Mrs. Charlston, digs in her nose—*a lot*; Mr. Pickle, my math teacher, practically has waterfalls falling out of his mouth when he talks; and my science teacher—well, let's just say she is in a group of her own when it comes to weird.

All the classrooms at my elementary school had tall wooden cabinets lined up along the back. Most of my teachers kept dodge balls and construction paper in them; I was allowed to go inside them at any time, but my science class, that was a different story. My science teacher, Ms. Gavin, made sure to always keep them locked. I had never thought anything of it before, until I noticed that Ms. Gavin would freeze in her tracks whenever someone went near them. Once, just to test her, I decided to pretend that there was something in the cabinets that I needed.

"Ms. Gavin," I said, walking toward the back of the classroom, "I think I need some more paper from the cabinets."

"No, you don't!" I heard her say quickly, in a worried tone of voice. "The construction paper is right here." I remember that she held up a few pieces of colorful paper to prove to me that there was nothing that I needed in the cabinets. Her eyes had grown wide, and the paper that she held up made flapping sounds as it shook in her hands.

"No," I said, continuing to walk toward the cabinets. "Those aren't the colors I want. I think there might be some in here," I said while reaching my hand out to the knob of the cabinet door. But before I could touch it, Ms. Gavin was in front of me, with her arms spread out and her back pressed against the cabinets.

"There is no construction paper in here," she said through clenched teeth, trying to keep her voice low.

I took one look at her narrowed eyes and instantly turned to walk back to my seat. *Yup, I remember saying to myself when I sat down in my seat. There is definitely something in those cabinets!*

"Okay," I heard my mother's voice say, snapping me out of my thoughts as she pulled up in front of my school and slowly brought the car to a stop. "Have a great day at school."

"I will," I said as I unbuckled my seatbelt. I leaned over to the driver's side of the car and gave her a quick kiss on the cheek before jumping out.

"Bye," I said, shutting the door and rushing up the stairs to my school. I walked into the hallway, where there were colorful posters of smiling students that I didn't know posted all over the walls. I had ten minutes to get to class, so I decided to stop by the bathroom. As I entered the girls' restroom, I walked over to the sink, looked in the mirror, and ran my fingers through my neatly braided hair. I brushed the crumbs from the donuts that I'd had for breakfast off my brown-sugar face. The bell rang for class to begin, and I sighed as I looked at myself in the mirror. First stop, Ms. Gavin's science class. Sometimes it was a complete drag to have her class first, but other times I was glad to get her out of the way. I walked out of the restroom and down the hall to Ms. Gavin's room. All of the students were rushing past me and into the classroom to take their seats. I walked slowly to my desk near the front of the class and placed my lime-green Princess Tiana backpack on the side of my desk. I pulled my matching notebook and pen out of my backpack and set them out in front of me.

"Okay, class," Ms. Gavin said, standing in front of her desk. "Settle down so that we may begin," she continued as she pulled out a textbook. Her jet-black hair was brushed back into a tight bun, and she wore glasses with thick, black rims. Her nose was pointy like a bird's beak, and her legs were long; she wore black slacks and a red button-up blouse that made her pale skin seem pink. The class began to quiet down, as Ms. Gavin flipped through the pages of her textbook. "Okay," she began, still looking inside her book—but at the sound of something crashing to the floor, Ms. Gavin's head shot up quickly to see what had happened. I turned to the back of the class to see Brian Rogers picking up the marbles he had dropped all around his desk—and near the cabinets.

"Brian!" Ms. Gavin shrieked, her eyes becoming wide.

Brian looked up, a couple of inches away from one of the cabinet doors. "Yeah?"

"Get away from the cabinets," she said nervously.

Brian looked at her and smirked. "What about my marbles?" He looked back down at his rolling marbles and continued to pick them up.

"Brian!" Ms. Gavin shouted again, sounding even angrier than before. "Get. Away. From. The. Cabinets." Her voice was low and scary, and she made sure to say each word clearly.

"I need to pick up my marbles," Brian said, not paying Ms. Gavin any attention. At that, Ms. Gavin slammed her book shut and dropped it to the floor. She marched to the back of the classroom with the eyes of all of the students following her. She walked behind Brian and picked him up by his arms, placing him roughly in his seat. Brian's eyes became big, as he looked up at her with his bottom lip dropping open.

"Stay in your seat," she ordered before she walked back toward the front of the class. I watched her as she picked her textbook up off the floor and opened it again.

"Okay, class," she said, continuing on as if nothing had happened. "Turn to page 93 in your textbooks, please." She turned her back to us and walked over to the board. I looked back at Brian, whose body seemed to be shivering as he began turning pages in his book. I turned back to Ms. Gavin, who was quickly writing something on the board, and then I looked back at the cabinets. I was now 100 percent positive that there was something behind those cabinet doors, and I was also 100 percent positive that I was going to find out what it was.

Chapter 2

"Vanessa!" my mother yelled as I was finishing the last problem of my math homework. "Are you ready?"

"Almost!" I yelled back.

I slipped my white tennis shoes onto my feet and pulled my favorite black sweatshirt with purple and gold butterflies printed on the front over my head. My hair was done in neat individual braids that fell just below my shoulders, and I pulled them back into a ponytail. I patted off my jeans and ran to the front door to meet my mother.

"Ready," I said as my mother grabbed her coat from the coat rack.

"Good," she said, slipping it on. "I don't want to be late for your back-to-school night."

She zipped up her coat, grabbed her keys, and walked behind me out the door and to the car.

"So," my mother began as she pulled the car out of the driveway and onto the street. "Tell me about some of your teachers."

"Well," I said as I sat back in my seat. "My homeroom teacher picks her nose whenever we have a test, because she thinks we're not looking."

"Interesting."

"No, Mom, I don't think you understand; I mean, she *really* picks her nose. It's like she's digging for a lot more than gold."

"Oh, stop," my mother said, smiling.

"I never knew someone's finger could go that far up their nose. It's like her fingernails are on a road trip !"

By this time my mother was bursting with laughter.

"I'm just saying that if she tries to shake your hand, don't. Who knows what else she does when she's *alone*."

"You're too much," my mother said, not taking her eyes off the road.

"My math teacher spits when he talks. It's like we're going to have a flash flood every day in class. I'm thinking that I should wear a raincoat when I go to class from now on."

"You are not," my mom said with a smirk.

"And my science teacher, well, she's just plain weird."

"Well, that isn't very nice, Vanessa."

"No, but it's very true. Just look out for her. She is definitely 'cuckoo for Cocoa Puffs.' You just wait and see."

~ ~ ~

A few minutes later my mother pulled into Book Smith Elementary School. The parking lot was filled with cars. I watched as parents walked up the steps to the school with their kids by their sides.

"Okay," my mom said, pulling the car into a parking spot. "Let's go meet these interesting teachers of yours."

"Let's," I said, unbuckling myseat belt and getting out of the car.

We made our rounds to most of my classes. I had to hand my mom a tissue to wipe her face after she had finished talking to my math teacher.

"Told ya," I said with a smirk as I skipped to my next class.

But I did give her a thumbs-up as she left my homeroom teacher's class, when I saw that she had pretended to drop something when my teacher tried to shake her hand.

"Last, but not least," I said, leading the way to my science class.

When we got there, all of the parents were seated, with their kids seated next to them, while Ms.

Gavin was leaning against the front of the desk facing the class. After my mother and I took our seats, Ms. Gavin began.

"Hello everyone, and welcome to my class," she said, standing stiffly with her arms folded in front of her, showing almost no emotion on her face. "I am the science teacher for the fifth-grade students of Book Smith Elementary School." She sounded almost robotic, as if she had practiced saying that in the mirror a thousand times before she came here tonight. As I listened to her dry speech, I began to get a little hot, as if she had the heater on or something. I took off my sweatshirt and placed it on the back of my chair. Ms. Gavin went on about the different things that she taught; I began to tune her out, as I took quick glances at the cabinets behind me.

"Pay attention," my mother whispered to me, tugging on my shirt. I turned around, pretending to listen as Ms. Gavin continued on with her boring speech. I smiled as I saw Brandon Thorton and his dad yawn at the same time. Then, on the other side of the room, I saw Liz Bryman's mom nodding off to sleep in her chair. A loud giggle escaped from my mouth, and half the room turned in my direction—including my mother, with a not-so-happy glare. I covered my smile with my hands and looked down toward the floor.

"Are there any questions?" Ms. Gavin asked, looking around at everyone in the class.

"Nope!" Lynne Sherman's father said, jumping out of his chair; when everyone turned to look at him, he quickly sat back down.

"Well, okay, I guess that's it," Ms. Gavin said, clapping her hands together. "Have a good night." She walked around her desk to the board and began to erase her name. All the parents got up from their chairs and walked out of the classroom, with me and mom following behind.

"I have to say," my mother said as she jumped into the driver's side of the car. "Your science teacher seems to be the sanest of them all. Boring, but sane," she said, putting her seatbelt on. I shook my head, as I began to put my seatbelt on as well, but I froze when

I realized that I had forgotten to grab my sweatshirt when I left Ms. Gavin's class.

"Oh Mom, I forgot my sweatshirt! I have to go get it; I'll be back," I said, jumping out of the car and running up the stairs to the school. I pushed past all the parents and students leaving the school and headed for Ms. Gavin's room.

When I got there, the door was shut. The last thing I needed was for it to be locked. I wanted my sweatshirt—who knew what she would do with it. I put my hand on the knob and slowly turned. I was relieved to find that it wasn't locked. I slightly opened the door and looked inside. The room was pitch black. I couldn't see a thing. I stepped in, careful not to make a sound. I couldn't find the light switch in the darkness, so I decided to just feel my way to where my sweatshirt was. But I froze when I heard footsteps walking near the classroom. I don't know why, but I panicked, and I crawled under Ms. Gavin's desk. About a second later, I heard the door open and the footsteps walk in. I caught my breath as Ms. Gavin's feet appeared in front of me below the desk. I was puzzled when I noticed that she hadn't turned on the classroom lights; she seemed to be finding her way through the room with a flashlight. I watched as her feet followed the light to the back of the classroom. I laid on the ground stiffly, with the palms of my hands toward the cold, hard floor. I heard jiggling noises, as if she were fiddling with her keys, or something. After a few moments I heard a click, and then I heard the slow turning sound of one of the cabinet doors being opened. "Hello, my babies," I heard Ms. Gavin say.

My babies? I said to myself. Who was she talking to?

"You're almost ready."

Who's *almost ready?*

"Just a few more weeks," I heard her say.

I was completely creeped out! I had to get out of there. As she continued to talk, I began to slowly slide from under the desk. I stood up quietly and tiptoed toward the door. When I reached the knob, I slowly turned it and squeezed out of the slightly opened door. I quietly closed the door and ran like the wind, down the hall, and out of the school. My mother's car was one of the last cars in the lot.

When I reached the car, I jumped in, breathing heavily, and put on my seatbelt.

"What took you so long?" my mother asked, looking at me strangely.

"The door was locked; I couldn't find anyone to open it. I'll just get my sweatshirt tomorrow."

"Okay," my mother said as she started up the car and left the parking lot. I didn't relax until the school was completely out of sight.

Chapter 3

The next day, when the bell rang for class to begin, I stood in front of Ms. Gavin's classroom door before walking in. I took a deep breath, as the kids shoved past me into the classroom. When I finally entered, I walked slowly to my desk. I sat down at my desk and looked back toward the area where my mom and I had sat last night. I wasn't surprised to see that my sweatshirt was nowhere in sight. I exhaled and turned around to see Ms. Gavin's tall figure standing right in front of my desk.

"Hello, Vanessa," she said, looking over the rim of her thick, black glasses, her sharp, pointed nose staring down at me. I looked up at her and swallowed.

"Hello, Vanessa," she said again, her lips in a flat line.

"H-hi," I stammered, looking up at her, my nails scratching the table of my desk.

Busted! I thought. She knew that I had seen her last night. She had to have heard me when I ran down the hall. Now I was in big trouble. I lowered my head and looked down at my hands, waiting for her to tell me that she knew I had been hiding under her desk.

"You left this last night," she said, holding out a black folded piece of clothing. I looked up at it and slowly took it from her. I held it in my hands and ran my fingers over the purple and gold butterflies that were on the front.

"Th-thank you," I said, looking up at her.

I watched as she put her hands behind her back and swiftly turned and walked back toward her desk.

"Okay, class," Ms. Gavin said, turning around to face us. "Take out your books and turn to the review section of chapter 5."

I closed my eyes and exhaled deeply. I looked around at the other kids taking out their books. I followed along and looked up at Ms. Gavin as she began her lesson. As I pulled out my notebook, I looked back toward the cabinets and then back at Ms. Gavin. I looked down at my notebook and tried to follow along as well as I could, but the only thing that I could think about was those tall brown doors behind me.

~ ~ ~

After my math class it was time for recess. I grabbed a snack out of my backpack and found my two friends, Dena and Mason, playing on the swing set outside. "Hey," I said, walking up to them.

"Hey," they said back in unison, swinging on the swing set. "Ms. Gavin was so-o-o boring last night at the teacher conferences!" Dena yelled as she continued to swing.

"I know!" I said, giving a smirk. "And I definitely feel like she has something in the cabinets!"

Mason rolled his eyes as he jumped off the swing. "You always say that."

"Well, it's true!" I said, becoming defensive.

"Sure, it is," Mason said, bending to tie his shoe.

There were times when I really wanted to kick him. "It is!" I yelled again. "Last night I heard her talking to something inside the cabinets. She called them her *babies*." I said the word as if it had grape soda and salt on it, the two things that I hated most in the world.

"Maybe she has puppies in there," Dena said as she kicked her feet back and forth.

"No," I said, shaking my head, "If there were puppies, we would have heard them by now. She's keeping something else in there, and we have to figure it out."

"*We?*" Dena said, burying her feet in the sand to bring her swinging to a quick stop.

"Yeah. We have to find out what she's keeping in there."

Mason stood up from the sand and dusted off his pants. "*We* don't have to do anything. You're the one who claims that there's something there. Why do you need us?"

"Because I don't want to do it by myself. What if it's something ... gross?"

"Well, that's for you to find out and then tell us, because I'm not about to go through anyone's cabinets. If I wanted an adventure, I'd watch the Discovery Channel," Dena said, standing up from the swing and walking away across the sand.

"Yeah, Dena's right," Mason said. "You're on your own with this one."

"Hey! Last one to the snack bar is a rotten egg!" Dena screamed as she began running in the direction of the cafeteria.

"You cheater!" Mason yelled, chasing after her.

I pouted my lips as I watched them both run away.

"Some friends," I said as I walked over to the swing and began to pump my legs back and forth. I really didn't want to break into Ms. Gavin's cabinets by myself. I guessed now that I would never know what Ms. Gavin was keeping in there. I began to pump my legs harder on the swing, but then I had to dig the toes of my tennis shoes into the sand to bring myself to a screeching stop.

"I'll help you!" A little chocolate-coated boy said from in front of me.

"You'll help me do what?" I asked, confused.

"Break into the cabinets! I got yo' back!"

I looked at him and snorted. "How old are you?" I asked him.

"I'll be nine in six months," he said with a huge smile.

I closed my eyes and shook my head; there was no way I was going to have an eight-year-old help me get into Ms. Gavin's cabinets. "What's your name?"

"Jonathan Jermaine Johnson. But you can just call me Johnny."

"Well, Johnny, it's been great meeting you, but I don't think I'm going to need your help," I said, putting a hand on his shoulder.

"Of course you will. I know this school inside and out. Plus, you're going to need me to protect you."

"*Protect* me?" I said, drawing back. "But you're only eight."

"Come on," he said. "Give me the menifit of the out."

"Don't you mean the *benefit* of the *doubt*?" I said with my eyebrows raised.

"Whatever! Look, I can do this; I just watched that new karate movie, you know, the one with Bill Swift's son. I watched it four times; I know every move. Watch!"

I watched as Johnny broke into his own wild version of the karate movements that he had seen in the movie.

"Woo yah!" he shouted as he extended out his left palm and pulled in his right fist. "Ha cha!" He yelled again as he shot his leg in the air. "Woooooo yaaaaaah," he bellowed as he began swinging his arms in a windmill-like rotation.

"Bi yah!, Boo yah! Nah Cha! Do—"

"Okay!" I yelled, not able to take it anymore. Kids were pointing and staring, and I just desperately wanted him to stop. "Okay, you can help me."

"Yes!" he screamed, pumping his fist in the air. "Oh yeah, oh yeah," he said as he did a weird dance.

"People are staring at you," I said, becoming embarrassed again.

"They don't want none of this!" Johnny said, thumping his hands on his chest like a gorilla. I wanted to bury myself in the sand beneath me as he began to do his karate movements again. "Bo bo bo," he said, running up to the top of a nearby picnic table. "Hey, kid!" he yelled, pointing his finger at a boy across the playground. Startled, the boy looked toward Johnny. "You want some of this!?" Johnny screamed.

The boy looked at Johnny, confused, and then picked up his ball and ran away.

"That's what I thought!" Johnny yelled after the boy.

"Oh, Johnny," I said, covering my face with my hands.

"When?" Johnny said, jumping off the table.

"When what?" I said, lifting my head up.

"When are we breaking into the cabinets?"

I sat quietly for a second, trying to think of a good time, and then I realized that my mom would be working late tonight and Mrs. Rubert would be babysitting me. It never failed that not long after my mother left Mrs. Rubert would fall into a deep sleep onto the couch, for hours. I practically watched myself.

"Tonight?"

"Tonight it is, then. I'll meet you on the side of the school at 7:00. I only live around the corner."

"Okay."

"And my services aren't for free."

"Your services!" I yelled, shocked by his words.

"Yup, and you have to sign my contract."

"Contract!" I said, even more shocked. *Who does this kid think he is?*

"Yup," he said, going into his Spiderman backpack; a few seconds later he pulled out a folded piece of construction paper that had a list of things written in green crayon.

I took the wrinkled piece of paper and read over the list.

Johnnyies conract

1. Johnny is the boss
2. Johnny ~~gits~~ gets payd one packet of watermelon gum every hour
3. Johnny is the first to enter asigneded target
4. Johnny is the first to leave in a emarguncie
5. Johnny is always ~~write~~ right
6. When the mision is over, costomor must not ever talk to Johnny
7. Costomer must agree that Johnny is one bad brutha

   +_____

I stood there looking at the paper in my hand. He couldn't be serious, could he? He pulled out a green crayon from his pocket and held it out to me.

"I need you to sign it, please," he said with a big smile.

I rolled my eyes, as I took the crayon out of his hands and signed my name on the line. "There," I said, pushing it back out to him.

"Thanks!" he said excitedly, putting the contract and crayon away in his backpack. "I'll see you tonight!"

I stood there in the sand, watching Johnny run away. *Tonight!* I thought to myself. I had wanted to get this done soon, but for some reason tonight seemed too soon. I was snapped out of my thoughts by the recess bell. I picked my backpack up off the ground and began to walk toward my last class. Tonight was the night.

Chapter 4

Just as I had predicted, my mom was gone and Mrs. Rubert was laid out in front of the TV, snoring loudly. I sat at the dining room table, finishing up some homework as I created a habit of checking the clock every two minutes. When 6:45 p.m. came around, I grabbed my sweatshirt, tiptoed over to the front door, and left the house.

At exactly 7:00 I arrived at the school. The parking lot was empty. I scurried over to the side of the school and hid behind a dumpster. I looked around me and began to take steps backward to make sure that I wasn't being followed. I took slow steps backward and nearly jumped out of my skin when I heard a voice from behind me.

"You're late."

Shivering, I turned to meet Johnny, who was standing with his arms folded in front of him. "You scared the bejeebers out of me!" I yelled at him.

"And you're late," he repeated again.

"You said to be here at 7:00 p.m.," I said, annoyed.

"Yeah, and its 7:01 p.m.," he said, pointing at his red Iron Man digital watch on his left wrist. I rolled my eyes and shook my head.

"Whatever. Can we just do this before we get caught?"

"Did you bring the goods?" he said, looking up at me.

I rolled my eyes and searched my pocket for the watermelon-flavored Bubblicious gum that I had brought for him. "Here," I said, handing it to him.

"Thank you," he said with a smile as he dropped the gum into his pants pocket. I took this opportunity to look him over. He wore a black hooded sweatshirt with matching black pants. He had on black shoes and, I was pretty sure, black socks. Each of his cheeks had one thick black stripe marked on it, like those football players on TV.

"What are you wearing?" I said with a snort.

He looked me up and down before he spoke.

"What are *you* wearing, amateur!" he said before he walked away from me and closer to the school.

I looked down at my blue jeans and white Converse shoes; I wore my favorite sweatshirt and my hair was in a ponytail. This was going to be a long night. I caught up to Johnny and grabbed his arm. "You don't even know where you're going; my teacher's class is this way," I said, pointing in the opposite direction. I turned around and began walking toward Ms. Gavin's class. After we had passed a few classroom windows, I began to slowly tiptoe over to

Ms. Gavin's window. I placed my hands on the glass and peeked inside.

"That's it," I said, pointing toward the back of the dark classroom as I felt Johnny walk up beside me. "Those are the cabinets."

"Target marked," Johnny said, on his tippy-toes with his nose pressed up against the glass. I looked at him, rolled my eyes, and then looked back toward the cabinets. As I stared at them, I wanted to kick myself as I realized I hadn't thought of one major detail.

"How are we going to get in?" I said, groaning.

I heard Johnny exhale loudly. "Follow me," he said, in a tone that made me feel as if he were two years older than me and not the other way around.

Curious, I followed; he was walking in the direction he had been walking before. Once we got in front of a certain window, Johnny ran to pick up something that was leaning against the wall.

"What is that?" I asked, trying to look around to see what it was he was picking up.

He turned to face me, holding a big orange and green water gun in his hands.

"You brought a water gun!" I yelled, dropping to my knees in laughter. "*What* do you think this *is?*" I said between laughs that had my stomach doing flips with pain. I couldn't control the tears that rolled down my face. After a few seconds I began to calm down, and I looked up at Johnny from the ground. That was when I got a big shot of water right in the face. "Hey!" I said, jumping to my feet.

"No, *you* hey!" Johnny said. "What do *you* think this is? In case you didn't know, this is a top-flight mission, and I'm not taking any chances."

"All right, already," I said, wiping my face. "I just thought it was a little funny." As I continued to wipe my face with my hands, I licked my lips and tasted something a little *different* about the water.

"Did you put salt in your water gun?"

"*And,*" he said, ignoring my question and continuing on with his rant, "This isn't just a water gun."

"What is it, then?" I asked, just for amusement.

"It's an Exosquirt 3000, and it can squirt up to ten feet. Any more questions?"

"No," I said. I just wanted to get this night over with.

"Good," he said, turning around and walking back toward the spot where he had retrieved the water gun. "Oh, and another thing," he said, turning back to face me.

"What," I asked, annoyed.

"If the cops come, you're taking the fall. I have a reputation to protect."

"Reputation?" I asked, confused. But Johnny had already turned around and was walking back toward the classroom window, placing the strap from his toy gun over his back. I walked up behind him and watched as he pushed up the window far enough for us to get into the classroom.

Wide-eyed, I asked, "How did you do that!"

"I put a pencil in the window before school was over today."

"Wow, that was pretty smart."

"That's why they pay me the big bucks."

This would have been another great moment to roll my eyes, but I just wanted to get inside. I pushed Johnny to the side and began to pull my leg up to the windowsill.

"Wait a minute, my sistah!" Johnny said, knocking my leg back to the ground.

"Johnny *always* goes first." He shoved me to the side. He struggled as he tried his best to pull his leg high enough to reach the windowsill. "Give me some help, here."

I smirked as I picked him up by the back of his sweat jacket and roughly pushed him inside the class. I clenched my eyes shut, and I heard Johnny's high-pitched scream come to a screeching stop as he hit the classroom floor.

"Sorry," I said as I peeked into the classroom.

"Yeah, yeah," he said, pulling himself up to his feet.

I put all my weight on the windowsill and lifted my feet up off the ground, pulling my body in through the open window. I allowed my feet to hit the ground and then looked around at the dark classroom.

"So this is your class?" I asked.

"Yup," Johnny said with a lot of excitement. "Want to see my drawing for art—my teacher put it on the board."

"Maybe later. We need to get to my class," I said, walking toward the door that would lead to the hallway.

"Oh yeah," I heard him say from behind me. "But wait!" he yelled grabbing the back of my sweatshirt.

"What?" I said, turning around.

"You should let me go first."

"Okay," I said, allowing him to walk in front of me.

"Oh yeah," he said as he remembered something else. He dug into his pocket and pulled out two blue miniature-size keychain flashlights. "Take one."

Another smart idea, I mused, as I took one out of his hands and turned it on. Maybe Johnny was more helpful than I'd thought.

When we got to the door, we opened it slowly and poked our heads out into the hall.

"Clear," Johnny said from underneath me, as he pushed the door open wider, holding his water gun in front of him. I watched him as he kept his body low, running down the hall. I lowered my body and did the same.

I followed close behind Johnny, but I paused when he stopped running down the hall and hurried to press his back up against the wall.

"What are you doing?" I asked, staring at him.

"Shhh!" he said as he began to move slowly, sliding his back against the wall. Then he stopped, got down, rolled across the hallway floor, and pressed his back against the opposite wall.

"Oh, Johnny," I groaned. I carried on walking toward my classroom as Johnny continued his rolling behind me.

A moment later, we arrived at my class. "This is it," I said, holding onto the doorknob.

"Well, what are you waiting for?" I heard Johnny say as he ran up to me.

I took a deep breath and turned the knob. I slowly opened it and moved to the side, as Johnny pushed past me to go inside.

"So this is it," Johnny said, looking around the room.

"Yeah," I said, not taking my eyes off the cabinets. I walked past the desk and to the cabinets. I pulled the little knob, but I wasn't surprised to find that it was locked. "They're locked," I said out loud.

"Of course," Johnny said, walking over with a small silver object in his hands.

"What is that?" I asked

"A safety pin," he answered as he fidgeted with the safety pin and the lock. After a few seconds, I heard a click, and Johnny stepped back. "Done."

"I don't even want to know where you learned that," I said, shaking my head. I placed my hand on the small knob of the cabinets.

I pulled the knob slowly, and my eyes widened at what I saw lying behind that cabinet door.

"Ooooooh, man," Johnny said standing next to me. "I didn't sign up for this!"

"What is it?" I said, not able to take my eyes off it. My heart began to pound harder in my chest, and my body began to shake.

"What have you gotten us into?"

"I-I don't know," I stuttered, closing my eyes as if I would be able to erase what was in front of me.

"Well then," Johnny said, with an unusually cheery attitude for the situation at hand. "Since you don't know what it is, and I don't know what it is, I say we lock this cabinet back up and go outside to play flashlight wars."

"Just wait," I said, when I finally felt the breath coming back to my body. I stared wide-eyed at the giant eggs in front of me.

There were four of them, perched next to each other, all of them taller than me. They were brown, with even darker brown specks on them, and they were about as wide as the classroom door. There were thick spider webs all around them, and they each had a reddish-tinted glow coming from inside. I slowly stretched my hand out and placed it on the red glow that I couldn't take my eyes off. It was steaming hot. I quickly snatched my hand back and looked at my red palm.

"Well, that was dumb," I heard Johnny say.

"Shut up," I said, shaking my hand from the pain.

"How'd you get to the fifth grade?"

"Shut up!" I said, rubbing my palms together.

"They must be letting anyone in nowadays."

"Shut up!" I yelled at him. Then I watched as the egg that I had touched slowly began to shake.

Johnny whipped his water gun around in front of him and began to squirt the egg. But he stopped after he saw that his water seemed to be acting like acid on the egg's shell. Steam rose into the air, and the part of the shell that he had squirted began to crack. As we watched the egg, we both jumped back, as it began to rumble. "O-o-o-kay, time to go," Johnny said, wide-eyed. He quickly turned away from the cabinets.

"Yeah, I think you're right," I said, quickly closing the cabinet doors. "Wait!" I said, stopping Johnny in his tracks as he was halfway out the classroom door. "We need to lock it!"

Johnny closed his eyes and ran back over to the cabinets, inserting his safety pin into the lock. "Please don't eat me, please don't eat me, please don't eat me," I heard Johnny say under his breath as he fidgeted with the small lock. After I heard a click, I watched as Johnny dropped the safety pin and made a beeline for the door.

Taking one last look at the cabinets, I dashed after Johnny.

"Wait, Johnny!" I yelled, trying to keep up with him. But he was already far ahead of me and turning the corner to his classroom.

I ran faster, so that he wouldn't completely disappear, and I entered the classroom just a few seconds after Johnny. He pulled himself onto the windowsill quickly—without my help—and leaped out of the window. I followed behind him and jumped out onto the grass, breathing heavily. Johnny ran over and pulled the window back down.

"What *was* that?" I exclaimed, breathing heavily.

"What was what?" Johnny asked. He looked confused and was breathing just as hard as I was.

"Those things in the cabinets!" I said, pointing toward the school.

"I didn't see nothing," Johnny said, waving his hand. "I didn't see nothing, I don't know nothing, and as far as I know, I'm not even here." He ranted on as he walked away from me. "I don't even think I'm a student at this school. Doesn't look familiar to me."

I shook my head as Johnny walked off in the opposite direction, toward his home, rambling on and on to himself. But Johnny was right. I didn't know anything about what was going on in those cabinets—and I didn't want to know. That was all for Ms. Gavin. I didn't want to know anymore why she was so secretive; I didn't want to know why there were eggs *that* size in *that* cabinet, and I was absolutely and positively sure that I didn't want to know what was in them!

Chapter 5

Iraced home and sneaked in the front door. Mrs. Rubert was asleep on the couch in front of the TV. I walked quickly past the living room and over to my mother's office. I closed the door behind me and quickly booted up the computer. When the homepage greeting my mother came up, I hurriedly typed in the web address Pow.com, a search engine that I used a lot while doing my homework. When the website came up, I typed in the phrase, *large eggs*, but the only big eggs that continued to pop up were ostrich eggs. The article said that they weighed about three pounds, and they looked about as big as the head on one of my life-size baby dolls. As interesting as they were to read about, those were definitely not the eggs that we had seen in Ms. Gavin's cabinets. Upset at not having found out what could have been in those eggs, I turned off the computer and left my mother's office. As I was walking up the stairs, I heard my mother come in through the door.

"Hello, Mrs. Rubert," I heard my mother say. From the staircase, I watched her walk into the living room.

"Oh!" I heard Mrs. Rubert say, probably waking up at the sound of my mother's voice.

"How was Vanessa?"

"A doll, as usual."

"Thank you again for watching her."

"Anytime, dear."

I allowed them to have their little chitchat, as I continued up the stairs to my room. When I got there, I let myself fall face forward on my unmade bed. Tomorrow was Friday, so maybe I could fake a couple of coughs and stay home from school. Mom worked from home on Fridays, anyway, so she wouldn't have to worry about anyone watching me. I just knew that I needed a break from that place. I didn't want to be anywhere near those cabinets anymore! Whoever said curiosity was a good thing should have Play-Doh thrown at them. My thoughts were interrupted by the knock at my door.

"Knock, knock," I heard my mother say as she slightly pushed my door open.

"Come in," I said in a low voice, turning my body around to face her as I reached for the teddy bear that was lying next to me.

"How are you?"

Now was my chance; I needed to put a few good coughs out, and then I would be home free. "Ahem, ahem. I'm okay. Ahem, ahem—I just feel a little dizzy," I said with the saddest voice I possibly could.

"Save it," my mother said from the foot of my bed. "You're going to school tomorrow."

"Ugh!" I said, turning my face back into my pillow.

"What's wrong?" I heard my mother chuckle. "Long day?"

"If only you knew," I said

"You can be so dramatic," my mother said, snatching my bear out of my arms and then throwing it at me. "I ordered a pizza. It should be here soon, so hurry up, get better, and get downstairs," she said as she left my room.

If only she knew.

Chapter 6

Ihesitated a little before I walked up the stairs to my school. As the kids ran past me to the entrance, I stood there staring blankly at the double doors. It wasn't until the school bell rang that I realized that I needed to get to class. Science, of course. I took a huge gulp before I jogged up the stairs behind everyone else. My heart fluttered before I turned the corner to my class. My palms began to sweat. *Everything is fine*, I said silently to myself as I walked into the room.

I walked slowly to my desk near the window, staring at the cabinets at the back of the room.

"You can sit down anytime now, Ms. Thomas," Ms. Gavin said, looking at me over the thick, black rims of her glasses. Her black hair was tied in a neat bun, her white blouse had brown coffee stains down the front, and her black skirt that stopped just below her knees had donut crumb stains on it. I hadn't noticed, but the entire class had already taken their seats and I was still just standing there.

"I'm sorry," I said as I took my seat

"All right," Ms. Gavin said firmly. "Clear your desks of all notes and books, and take out a pen and a blank sheet of paper. You're having a pop quiz."

I looked around as the class groaned, while they began to put away their notes and books. I exhaled as I slowly began to do the same. *Maybe what I saw last night wasn't real; maybe my eyes were playing tricks on me.* As I began to dismiss the thoughts of something being in that cabinet last night, I started to hear a cracking sound. I stopped putting my book away and looked around at the rest of the class, but no one else seemed to have noticed. I looked up at Ms. Gavin, but she was busy writing something on the board. I tried my best to pretend that the sound had never happened, and I began to pull out my pen and blank sheet of paper, when I heard the cracking sound again. This time it was louder. As I looked up at Ms. Gavin, I saw that she had frozen; she seemed to have heard the sound, that time. Her body began to tremble as she held the chalk in her hands. "It's too soon," I heard her whisper to herself. Puzzled, I turned my attention back to the cabinets, as the sounds began to multiply.

What did she mean by "It's too soon"? Before I could try to figure it out, there was a huge bump from within the cabinet doors. The kids sitting toward the back of the classroom screeched, as they jumped out of their seats. I was too afraid to move. After a second, there was another loud bump. The cabinet doors moved outward, but the doors still remained locked. Now more kids were screaming and jumping out of their seats. I looked at Ms. Gavin fearfully, as the bumping began to get louder and more intense.

"Do something!" I yelled at her. I watched as her eyes became wide and the color left her face.

"There's nothing I can do," she said, standing there stiffly. I looked at her, confused, as I felt my body begin to tremble. Just then, I heard a loud bump come from the single cabinet at the front of the classroom, right in front of me. I had forgotten all about that one. By the second bump against the door, I was out of my seat. I hadn't noticed before, but all of the students were practically huddled together in the middle of the classroom. The banging was getting louder now from all of the cabinets in the room; it was almost as if something were trying to break out. We all began to ease our way toward the exit—when all of the cabinet doors burst open at once! The kids began to scream, but I froze, as I watched the red eyes of four huge creatures. They were tall, and they stepped out of the cabinets. They stood up straight, like humans, and their green bodies were covered with dripping slime. Their feet were like crows' feet, only bigger. Their teeth were white and pointy, like a handful of sharp number-two pencils lined right up next to each other. Their arms were long, and their fingernails looked like wood; their veins showed throughout their bodies, going in crisscrosses on their green faces. They had wild black hair, like that of troll dolls—only these creatures didn't seem very playful.

As the monsters inched closer to us, I shoved my way out of the classroom first, as all the students fought to get through the door at the same time. *Forget what that stupid contract said—I needed to find Johnny,* I thought, quickly rushing down the hall toward his classroom. I needed to tell him what was happening, so that we could get out of there, but before I reached the corner to turn toward his class, a stampede of students turned the corner toward me, all screaming, as they ran past me in the direction of my class.

"No, not that way!" I yelled at them. The hallway became filled with students, screaming and running in all different directions. I watched as the creatures left my classroom and began to grab students up. My mouth dropped, as they began to snatch students by their shirts and drag them down the hall. I *really* needed to find Johnny!

Chapter 7

I picked up my speed and began running down the hall and around the corner toward Johnny's class. I pushed past all the students that were running in my direction. *What could they possibly be running from?* I thought. *All the monsters are in* my *classroom.* As I got closer to his class, I stopped in my tracks when I heard one familiar scream. I looked toward his room and braced myself against the hallway wall, as I saw Johnny burst through his classroom door with a high-pitched scream. His eyes were wide, as he took off running and screaming down the hall. I wanted to call after him, but the sight of the monster that came out of the classroom and followed quickly after Johnny caused the words to turn to mush in my mouth.

I began running down the hall in the opposite direction. My heart practically stopped in my chest when I felt something grab the back of my sweatshirt and lift me up in the air. "Aaaaaah!" I screamed as I came eye to eye with the disgusting slimy creature. But, after a few moments, its mean face began to soften, and it slowly put me back down. After my feet touched the ground, it let go of the back of my shirt, set its eyes on another student, and quickly left my side. What had happened? But I really didn't care—all I knew was that it had let me go, and now I was about to vanish out of sight. I ran to the girls' restroom and locked myself in a stall. I sat down near the toilet and tucked my head into my knees, covering my ears with my hands, trying to get rid of the sounds of the screaming students in the hall.

I sat still and silent for what seemed like forever, until I slowly decided to pull my hands away from my ears. Everything was quiet now—freakily quiet. I stood up from the floor and opened the door of my stall. I walked slowly to the bathroom door and peeked out. The hallway was empty; there wasn't a soul in sight. I opened the door wider and stepped out. Where was everyone?

I walked down the hallway slowly but froze as I heard the sounds nearby. I stooped to the floor and hid by the side of a water fountain. I stayed as quiet as I possibly could, and then I saw one of the monsters round the corner and make its way down the hall. I allowed it to walk a little farther before I began to follow it. It was walking toward the gym. When it got there, I watched it disappear through the door. Maybe that's where everyone was.

I approached the door and slowly pulled the knob open. I walked slowly through the double doors of the gym, following the green slime that the creature had left behind as it walked. The gym was dark and cold; I shivered as I ran my hands up and down my arms. As I walked further into the gym, I heard the echo of my steps. I continued to walk slowly, but I stopped when I felt some of the same green slime that was on the ground hit my forehead. I touched the thick, warm gunk and looked up to see where it had come from. My bottom lip dropped open, as I saw what I had missed when I'd walked through the door. Above me hung a ceiling full of life-size caterpillar cocoons; they were furry and white, and they all seemed to be dripping with slime.

"I want my mommy," I heard a small voice say. I looked up toward a little girl who was wrapped in the cocoon, dripping with slime. "Ooh," I said, looking up at her. "It will be okay."

"Master," I heard a slimy, slithering voice say from behind me.

My body began to shiver as I turned to the source of the creepy voice. In front of me stood ten slime-dripping creatures, with their shiny, sharp teeth very visible.

"Master?" I repeated, confused.

"Yes," one hissed as it stepped closer to me. "You are the one who created us."

"No, no, no," I said, backing up and shaking my hands in front of me. "You have me confused with someone else."

The monsters cocked their heads and then looked at each other as if they hadn't understood anything I said.

"But it was your touch that brought us to life; it was your touch that completed us. It is you we answer to."

"My touch?" I asked, confused—but then I remembered. I *had* touched one of the eggs, and my handprint had lingered afterward. So did that mean that they were now *mine*? What was I supposed to do with them? "S-so what does this mean?"

"That we do as you wish," one of the monsters answered.

"Anything?" I asked, shocked.

"Anything," they all answered in unison.

I was flattered. But I still was holding onto the idea that there was nothing I wanted more than for them to leave. This was all too much.

"Well," I began. "I appreciate the fact that you all want to do anything that I say, but I think I'd rather have you all le—"

"Vanessa!" My body jerked around at the sound of someone screaming my name. I looked up frantically toward the ceiling and saw Johnny's legs dangling from the sticky cocoon.

"Johnny!"

"Help me!"

"Okay," I said, turning back toward the monsters. "I want you to let him go!" I yelled, pointing my finger up toward Johnny. I looked around at all the students that were trapped, and I cringed as they all began to call my name.

"Vanessa!"

"Vanessa!

"Vanessa!"

"I want you to let all of them go!" I yelled.

"Yes, master," they answered in unison, and they began to pry the students free from the slimy green cocoon.

Johnny was the first to be freed, and he ran over to me. "We gotta take these monsters out!" he yelled as he got closer to me.

"No!" I yelled back. "This isn't a joke. We have to get out of here!" I grabbed him by the collar of his shirt and began to drag him toward the gym door.

"No way!" he said, trying to pull away. "We have to at least try, Vanessa; we have to try!"

I stopped and turned to him. Maybe he was right. What would happen if we left and these things got outside—what would they do to the city?

"Okay," I agreed. "But how are we going to do that?" I asked, looking around at the ten huge monsters that were continuing to free the students tangled in the webs.

"I don't know," Johnny said, looking around with me. "But maybe we should ask your teacher."

"Yes!" I yelled. She *was* the reason they were here. I looked around at all the faces, but I didn't see any of the teachers. "But I don't know where she is—"

"Well, I saw them slam my teacher into the cabinet; maybe your teacher is in your classroom cabinets."

"Let's go then!" I yelled, grabbing him by the wrist and pulling him out of the gym.

We ran down the hall and toward my classroom. When we entered the door, we heard soft moans coming from the cabinets. We ran to them and opened them to find Ms. Gavin, with her knees to her chest, covered in green gunk.

"Listen, lady!" Johnny said, shoving me to the side and angrily grabbing Ms. Gavin by her shirt collar. "You'd better—"

"Johnny, move," I said, pushing him away. I yelled at Ms. Gavin, "What did you do!"

Ms. Gavin looked at me with the saddest watery eyes, and she shook her head. "It wasn't supposed to be like this."

"What do you mean?" I asked her, confused.

"They were supposed to be mine!" she yelled at us; this time *her* eyes were angry.

Johnny pointed his finger in Ms. Gavin's face with an even angrier look than hers. "You are one crazy—"

"How do we get rid of them?" I demanded, cutting him off.

"It was you who touched them, wasn't it?" she asked, her voice becoming scary. "You just couldn't stay away, and now everything is ruined!"

I backed up as I saw that her face was becoming red from anger. "How do we get rid of them?" I asked again.

"I can't tell you that!" she snapped.

My eyes widened at her response. "What do you mean, you can't tell us?"

"I spent years trying to breed these creatures. I'm not going to let you destroy them."

"Lady!" Johnny yelled, taking over again, "You got less than a second to tell us how to get rid of these things, or you're about to come up missing!"

"I'm not telling you anything."

"Fine!" I yelled before Johnny could respond. "We'll figure it out. So you can kiss your precious *babies* good-bye! Let's go, Johnny," I said, walking away from the cabinets.

Johnny began to follow me, but then he stopped as if he'd remembered something else that he wanted to share with Ms. Gavin.

"When this is over," he said, looking at her, "I'm coming *back* for you."

Johnny walked away from her and came back to follow me.

"But be careful," I heard her say from behind me. Both Johnny and I turned to face her. She had a grin on her face that showed that she definitely knew exactly how to get rid of these monsters.

"Why?" I asked.

"If they find out that *you,* their master, doesn't want them, they will feel rejected. And they don't take rejection too well."

I flinched at her smile, before I turned to leave the classroom and stormed down the hall.

"So, what's our game plan?" Johnny asked, skipping on beside of me with his orange-and-white Iron Man light-up shoes.

"I don't know," I said, and I felt tears forming behind my eyes. "I don't know how to do this."

"Come on," Johnny said, running in front of me down the hall.

"Where are we going?" I asked, following him.

"To my class. I have to get my Exosquirt 3000."

"Oh, Johnny," I said as we continued to run. I tried to speed up as he ran faster toward his class. "Johnny!" I yelled. "Johnny, you can't fight these things off with water!" I yelled again before he disappeared into the room.

"Master!" I heard a slimy voice say from behind me. I stopped in my tracks and slowly turned, until the gooey monster was standing directly in front of me. "We've been looking for you," it said.

"Oh," I said looking around. "I was just … uh … running some errands."

"Master, why do you want to get rid of us?"

I looked at him, confused. "Wh-what do you mean?"

"I heard you talking. You don't want us anymore."

These monsters were smarter than I'd thought. I took a step back and gulped as I saw it inching closer to me. "If you don't want us," it said, grabbing me by the collar of my shirt, "Then we don't want you." It began to lift me up by the back of my shirt.

My breath caught in my throat as I looked at the anger-filled creature that had lifted me up to its eye level.

"Maybe we could talk about this over some coffee," I said, trying to force a smile. But when I heard the growl that it hid under its breath, my smile quickly fell, and it was replaced with a look of terror.

"Aye-yi-yi!" I said as I closed my eyes and braced myself for whatever was coming.

"Aaaaaah!" My eyes shot open at the sound of Johnny's voice coming from behind me. "Get your hands off of her!" I heard him say, and the monster dropped me to my feet as it decided to make Johnny its new target.

"Johnny, run!" I yelled. But Johnny didn't budge; he whipped his Exosquirt from behind his back and pointed it at the monster.

"I hope you're thirsty," Johnny said before he began to pump his water gun back and forth, allowing a ton of water to go squirting out toward the monster.

I covered my eyes with my hands, knowing all too well that the monster would knock the water gun out of Johnny's hand and do who-knows-what to him.

But when I heard the loud screams coming from someone other than Johnny, I uncovered my eyes.

The monster had somehow shrunk, and his legs seemed to be turning into pure slime. His screams sounded like cars that were skidding on the road. I shared a look with Johnny—he seemed to be a little confused at what was happening, as well. *The water.*

I thought maybe it was just like that movie in which the wicked witch of the west had melted when that Dorothy girl threw water on her. I scrambled to the water fountain that was right near the monster and began to push some of the water out toward it to see if it would continue to melt. I waited, but nothing happened. Maybe it wasn't the water, I thought—but something from Johnny's water gun had definitely caused this monster to melt.

"Squirt it again, Johnny!" I yelled. Johnny raised his water gun and squirted the monster in the face. This time its screams became louder, as one of its eyeballs rolled out of its socket and became a part of the green slime that was slowly running down its face.

"Ewwwwwww," I heard Johnny say. *Eww* was right, but I didn't have time to think about how gross it was to see the monster's second eyeball fall out of its socket and into the green slime that was now at my feet. I was desperately trying to figure out what was different about Johnny's water. And then it hit me—last night, when Johnny had squirted me in the face, I was sure I'd tasted salt in his water. And then when he'd squirted the egg, something strange had begun to happen to it. That had to be it!

"Johnny, is there salt in your water?" I asked frantically.

"I always put salt in my water; it's better for when you aim for the eyes," he said with a smirk. It might have been better against the eyes, but that was small stuff compared to getting rid of these creatures at our school!

"Quick, Johnny! To the cafeteria!" I said, running toward the school's kitchen.

"We got a school full of monsters, and you're thinking about lunch?" I heard him say behind me.

"Hurry, Johnny!" I turned the corner and burst through the cafeteria doors. I ran past all the tables and into the kitchen. I opened one of the closets and was delighted to see shelves full of all different types of seasoning—shelves full of salt. I began pulling out the bottles of salt and throwing them to the ground.

"Salt?" Johnny asked, watching confused.

"It's your water! It's the salt water that's going to kill them. We have to get as much as we can!" I said, throwing down all the bottles of salt I could find. "Quick, put them in bags—we have to take them to the other kids in the gym."

"Why?" Johnny said, looking at me with a raised brow.

"There's too many, Johnny; we are going to need help." I turned around and looked at his still-raised eyebrow and released a defeated sigh. "I'll tell them they have to call you Captain."

"Sold," Johnny said with a smile, as he began to stuff the bottles of salt into empty trash bags. When I'd finished clearing the shelves of all the salt, I ran over to a corner, where they had small bottles of water piled in buckets. "Hurry, Johnny! To the gym," I said, dragging the heavy bucket of water bottles out of the kitchen.

"I'm coming!" Johnny said, swinging the bag of salt over his shoulders as he pushed his way out of the door. We tried to walk as quietly as possible as we made our way toward the gym, but that didn't stop us from attracting the attention of one monster, which growled from behind us.

Johnny's eyes widened as he dropped his bag of salt. I gulped before I turned to meet the face of the very angry creature showing his very sharp teeth.

"Johnny," I whispered between clenched teeth, "Your water gun."

"Already ahead of you," Johnny said, putting his gun in front of him and walking toward the monster. "Don't hate me because I'm cute," Johnny said to it, inching closer. "Hate me because I'm about to whoop yo—"

"Johnny, hurry!" I screamed as I saw another monster emerge.

As Johnny watched the second one emerge, he began to squirt salt water toward both the monsters, which started to melt to the ground, steam rising to the air as their eyeballs rolled out of their heads.

"Let's go," I said, throwing the trash bag into Johnny's arms and pulling him in the direction of the gym.

Chapter 8

When we got to the gym, all of the students were huddled together in the corners, crying. "All right, everybody!" Johnny yelled, getting everyone's attention. "It's time to go to war!"

"I just want to go home!" a little boy cried from behind us.

"Well, you're not going home until these slimy green monsters have been illiminated!" Johnny shouted.

"Eliminated," I corrected

"Whatever," he said, rolling his eyes.

"We can't fight them!" one kid yelled from another corner.

"Yes, we can!" I said, stepping up. "I know what it takes. I know what we need to do. For some reason, they react badly to salt water, and this is how it's going to work. You'll all need to take a bottle of salt and a bottle of water and go out there and fight! We can do this; I believe in you." They all looked at me as if they were too afraid to believe the words that were coming out of my mouth.

"Look, everybody," I heard Johnny say. "This is our school, and we're not going to let some snot-nosed, googly-eyed monsters take control over it, are we?"

"I guess not," a little girl said, drying her tears.

"That's right!" Johnny said, getting louder. "I have a dream that one day the students of Book Smith Elementary School will be able to walk the halls without stepping in the green slime left behind by those creatures," he said, pointing toward the door. "We can—and we will—take our school back! Yes, we can! Yes, we can!" Johnny began to chant while pumping his fist up into the air. "Yes, we can!"

One boy jumped from his spot on the ground and began to join in with Johnny's chant: "Yes, we can!"

"Yes, we can!" another boy shouted, standing up from the ground. Before long, nearly all the students were standing up and joining in the chant. They all began to step forward, grab the bottles of water and the salt that we had packed, and make their way out into the hall.

After all the kids had left, I looked over to Johnny. "Are you ready?" I asked him.

"Not yet," he said, digging into his pocket for something. He pulled out a small black container filled with black liquid. He opened the cap and stuck his finger inside. He brought his finger up to my face and smeared the cool black liquid on both of my cheeks. He did the same to his own and placed the black container back into his pocket. Then he looked at me. "Now I'm ready," he said. He began to walk toward the gym door, with his Exosquirt 3000 in his hands, but I caught him by his shoulder.

"Hey, Johnny?"

"Yeah, Vanessa," he said, turning around.

"What are you?" I asked with a smirk on my face.

I watched him as he squinted his eyes in a very serious face as if he were preparing himself for the battle. "I'm *one bad brotha*," he declared.

Quickly, he turned around toward the exit. "Waaaaaaaah!" Johnny yelled, kicking the gym door open.

I watched from the doorway as he ran quickly down the hall, rolling on the ground and helping the students to attack six monsters that filled the hallway.

"Let's do this," I said to myself.

I saw a monster emerge from a corner, and I opened the cap of a water bottle that I held in my hands. I threw it in its face; a few seconds later I threw the open bottle of salt. As had happened with the others, its face began to fall apart, steam rising in the air. I ran down the hall and passed three little girls who were dumping multiple bottles of salt and water unto a monster, whose body turned to pure liquid on the hallway floor. I ran past one kid who was shaking the remains of all of his water onto a monster while another kid threw salt in the very same spot.

The hallway floor was covered in the remains of all the creatures that had once stood tall. I rounded the corner and came to a screeching stop as I nearly ran into one of the monsters. I looked up at it and began to back away.

"Shall I do the honors?" I heard a voice say from behind me.

I turned to see Johnny standing with his Exosquirt ready. All I could do was smile.

"Yes, you may," I said as I stepped to the side.

"Woooooooo! Waaaaaaaah!" Johnny cried and began to pump his squirt gun faster, spraying the salt and water all over the monster.

As the monster became slime, I smiled. I looked around to see all of the children jumping and cheering, with huge smiles on their faces, as they hugged and high-fived each other. The floor was covered in brownish-green slime, and it was safe to say that all the monsters were gone.

"We did it, Johnny!" I yelled, jumping over the green slime..

"I know!" he said, jumping up and down.

I looked around at all of the kids with a huge smile, but my smile slowly faded when I realized all the teachers were still probably locked away.

"Johnny, the teachers!" I shrieked.

"What about them?" he said, looking at me with both of his eyebrows raised.

"We have to go and get them, Johnny," I said, tilting my head to the side.

"Fine," he said, shaking his head. "But you know, I could have did without them."

"I know. But let's go."

Johnny ran to his classroom, and I followed behind him. "Help the teachers!" Johnny shouted at the other kids as he ran down the hall. The kids began to scatter around and into the classrooms.

When we got to Johnny's class, we ran toward the cabinets. He opened it up to find his teacher,

Ms. Larry, fully wrapped in white fuzz. We began to pull the fuzz off her, and her eyes slowly began to open.

"What ha-happened?" she said, pulling the white lint away from her face.

"Well," Johnny began. "There were these huge—"

"Nothing!" I said quickly when I realized Ms. Larry didn't remember anything that had happened.

"You were going into the cabinet for something, and you kind of ... uh ... fell. We were just helping you up."

"Oh," she said, still sounding a little confused, "Well, then thank you," she said, pulling herself up from the cabinets and dusting her blouse off. She looked at her watch and then looked at us. "It's 12:00—why aren't you both at lunch?"

I shared a look with Johnny and then turned back to Ms. Larry. "We were making our way there now," I said, pushing Johnny toward the door.

"Yup!" Johnny said excitedly. "We were on our way there now."

When we got to the hallway, all of the teachers were standing in the halls, scratching their heads and whispering to each other.

"What happened?" I heard one teacher say.

"What is all this stuff on the ground?" said another

Johnny and I made our way to my classroom and back to the cabinets. Johnny was the first to reach the open cabinet door, where Ms. Gavin was still stuck in the slime.

"I told you I was coming back," he grinned menacingly at her.

"What have you done?" she demanded, her eyes wide.

I started to pull the icky slime off her. "Why don't you go and look for yourself," I said with a smirk. After we had pulled the slime off, she quickly pulled herself up out of the cabinets.

She walked quickly toward the classroom door. She nearly melted herself when she saw all the green slime on the ground. "Noooooo!" she screamed. Johnny and I covered our mouths as we began to chuckle. She turned back to us frantically and then rushed over to her desk. She grabbed a black bag, threw the strap over her shoulder, and rushed quickly out the door.

"You little brats," she mumbled to herself. "All my hard work—ruined!" She continued to talk to herself as she made her way down the hall and to the school exit.

"Where are you going?" Principal Westler asked as he saw her about to leave the building.

"I quit!" she shouted loudly and pushed open the doors to the school parking lot.

"Ms. Gavin!" he yelled, chasing after her. "Ms. Gavin, wait!"

We ran behind Principal Westler and stood at the top of the school steps, watching Ms. Gavin jump into her car and speed off.

"Yes!" Johnny and I shouted in unison as we jumped up in the air.

We looked over at the other students, who were playing outside, eagerly talking about everything that had happened today.

"You think they'll tell their parents?" Johnny said, sitting down on the steps.

"Yup," I said, sitting down next to him.

"Do you think they'll believe them?"

"Not a chance," I said, shaking my head.

"I don't know why kids try these days," Johnny said, shaking his head along with me.

"It beats me." I turned to him and smiled. "We were pretty awesome today."

"Yeah," he said. "I think we work well together." He reached into his pocket and pulled out a wrinkled piece of paper. When he unfolded it, I saw that it was the contract that he had made me sign when we first met. I watched him pull out his green crayon and then write something on the paper.

"Now we're in business," Johnny said, showing me the paper. It was "Vanassa and Johnnyies Conract." I couldn't help but smile, even if he had spelled my name wrong.

"But there's one more thing," I said, taking the paper.

"What?" Johnny asked, confused.

"Customers must agree that Vanessa is *one bad sistah.*"

I doubled over laughing, with tears in my eyes. Johnny threw his head back, and placing his hand over his eyes, he laughed along with me.